DICK FRANCIS

RACING CLASSICS

PENGUIN BOOKS

PENGUIN BOOKS

Published by the Penguin Group. Penguin Books Ltd, 27 Wrights Lane, London W8 5TZ, England. Penguin Books USA Inc., 375 Hudson Street, New York, New York 10014, USA. Penguin Books Australia Ltd, Ringwood, Victoria, Australia. Penguin Books Canada Ltd, 10 Alcorn Avenue, Toronto, Ontario, Canada M4V 3B2. Penguin Books (NZ) Ltd, 182–190 Wairau Road, Auckland 10, New Zealand · Penguin Books Ltd, Registered Offices: Harmondsworth, Middlesex, England · This edition published 1995 · Typeset by Datix International Limited, Bungay, Suffolk. Printed in England by Clays Ltd, St Ives plc · 10 9 8 7 6 5 4 3 2 1

CONTENTS

Dead Cert: The First Chapter

The mingled smells of hot horse and cold river mist filled my nostrils. I could hear only the swish and thud of galloping hooves and the occasional sharp click of horseshoes striking against each other. Behind me, strung out, rode a group of men dressed like myself in white silk breeches and harlequin jerseys, and in front, his body vividly red and green against the pale curtain of fog, one solitary rider steadied his horse to jump the birch fence stretching blackly across his path.

All, in fact, was going as expected. Bill Davidson was about to win his ninety-seventh steeplechase. Admiral, his chestnut horse, was amply proving he was still the best hunter 'chaser in the kingdom, and I, as often before, had been admiring their combined back view for several minutes.

Ahead of me the powerful chestnut hindquarters bunched, tensed, sprang: Admiral cleared the fence with the effortlessness of the really great performer. And he'd gained another two lengths,

I saw, as I followed him over. We were down at the far end of Maidenhead racecourse with more than half a mile to go to the winning post. I hadn't a hope of catching him.

The February fog was getting denser. It was now impossible to see much farther than from one fence to the next, and the silent surrounding whiteness seemed to shut us, an isolated string of riders, into a private lonely limbo. Speed was the only reality. Winning post, crowds, stands, and stewards, left behind in the mist, lay again invisibly ahead, but on the long deserted mile and a half circuit it was quite difficult to believe they were really there.

It was an eerie, severed world in which anything might happen. And something did.

We rounded the first part of the bend at the bottom of the racecourse and straightened to jump the next fence. Bill was a good ten lengths in front of me and the other horses, and hadn't exerted himself. He seldom needed to.

The attendant at the next fence strolled across the course from the outside to the inside, patting the top of the birch as he went, and ducked under the rails. Bill glanced back over his shoulder and I saw the flash of his teeth as he smiled with satisfaction to see me so far behind. Then he turned his head towards the fence and measured his distance.

Admiral met the fence perfectly. He rose to it as if flight were not only for birds.

And he fell.

Aghast, I saw the flurry of chestnut legs threshing the air as the horse pitched over in a somersault. I had a glimpse of Bill's bright-clad figure hurtling head downwards from the highest point of his trajectory, and I heard the crash of Admiral landing upside down after him.

Automatically I swerved over to the right and kicked my horse into the fence. In mid-air, as I crossed it, I looked down at Bill. He lay loosely on the ground with one arm outstretched. His eyes were shut. Admiral had fallen solidly, back downwards, across Bill's unprotected abdomen, and he was rolling backwards and forwards in a frantic effort to stand up again.

I had a brief impression that something lay beneath them. Something incongruous, which ought not to be there. But I was going too fast to see properly.

As my horse pressed on away from the fence, I felt as sick as if I'd been kicked in the stomach myself. There had been a quality about that fall which put it straight into the killing class.

I looked over my shoulder. Admiral succeeded in getting to his feet and cantered off loose, and the attendant stepped forward and bent over Bill, who still lay motionless on the ground. I turned back to attend to the race. I had been left in front and I ought to stay there. At the side of the course a black-suited, white-sashed First Aid man was running towards and past me. He had been standing at the fence I was now approaching, and was on his way to help Bill.

I booted my horse into the next three fences, but my heart was no longer in it, and when I emerged as the winner into the full view of the crowded stands, the mixed gasp and groan which greeted me seemed an apt enough welcome. I passed the winning post, patted my mount's neck, and looked at the stands. Most heads were still turned towards the last fence, searching in the impenetrable mist for Admiral, the odds-on certainty who had lost his first race for two years.

Even the pleasant middle-aged woman whose

horse I was riding met me with the question 'What happened to Admiral?'

'He fell,' I said.

'How lucky,' said Mrs Mervyn, laughing happily.

She took hold of the bridle and led her horse into the winner's unsaddling enclosure. I slid off and undid the girth buckles with fingers clumsy from shock. She patted the horse and chattered on about how delighted she was to have won, and how unexpected it was, and how fortunate that Admiral had tripped up for a change, though a great pity in another way, of course.

I nodded and smiled at her and didn't answer, because what I would have said would have been savage and unkind. Let her enjoy her win, I thought. They come seldom enough. And Bill might, after all, be all right.

I tugged the saddle off the horse and, leaving a beaming Mrs Mervyn receiving congratulations from all around, pressed through the crowd into the weighing room. I sat on the scales, was passed as correct, walked into the changing room, and put my gear down on the bench.

Clem, the racecourse valet who looked after my

stuff, came over. He was a small elderly man, very spry and tidy, with a weatherbeaten face and wrists whose tendons stood out like tight strung cords.

He picked up my saddle and ran his hand caressingly over the leather. It was a habit he had grown into, I imagined, from long years of caring for fine-grained skins. He stroked a saddle as another man would a pretty girl's cheek, savouring the suppleness, the bloom.

'Well done, sir,' he said; but he didn't look overjoyed.

I didn't want to be congratulated. I said abruptly, 'Admiral should have won.'

'Did he fall?' asked Clem anxiously.

'Yes,' I said. I couldn't understand it, thinking about it.

'Is Major Davidson all right sir?' asked Clem. He valeted Bill too and, I knew, looked upon him as a sort of minor god.

'I don't know,' I said. But the hard saddle-tree had hit him plumb in the belly with the weight of a big horse falling at thirty miles an hour behind it. What chance has he got, poor beggar? I thought.

I shrugged my arms into my sheepskin coat and went along to the First Aid room. Bill's wife, Scilla, was standing outside the door there, pale and shaking and doing her best not to be frightened. Her small, neat figure was dressed gaily in scarlet, and a mink hat sat provocatively on top of her cloudy dark curls. They were clothes for success, not sorrow.

'Alan,' she said, with relief, when she saw me. 'The doctor's looking at him and asked me to wait here. What do you think? Is he bad?' She was pleading, and I hadn't much comfort to give her. I put my arm round her shoulders.

She asked me if I had seen Bill fall, and I told her he had dived on to his head and might be slightly concussed.

The door opened, and a tall slim well-groomed man came out. The doctor.

'Are you Mrs Davidson?' he said to Scilla. She nodded.

'I'm afraid your husband will have to go along to the hospital,' he said. 'It wouldn't be sensible to send him home without an X-ray.' He smiled reassuringly, and I felt some of the tension go out of Scilla's body.

'Can I go in and see him?' she said.

The doctor hesitated. 'Yes,' he said finally, 'but he's almost unconscious. He had a bit of a bang on the head. Don't try to wake him.'

When I started to follow Scilla into the First Aid room the doctor put his hand on my arm to stop me.

'You're Mr York, aren't you?' he asked. He had given me a regulation check after an easy fall I'd had the day before.

'Yes.'

'Do you know these people well?'

'Yes. I live with them most of the time.'

The doctor closed his lips tight, thinking. Then he said, 'It's not good. The concussion's not much, but he's bleeding internally, possibly from a ruptured spleen. I've telephoned the hospital to take him in as an emergency case as soon as we can get him there.'

As he spoke, one of the racecourse ambulances backed up towards us. The men jumped out, opened the rear doors, took out a big stretcher and carried it into the First Aid room. The doctor went in after them. Soon they all reappeared with Bill on the stretcher. Scilla followed, the anxiety plain on her face, deep and well founded.

Bill's firm, brown, humorous face now lolled flaccid, bluish-white, and covered with fine beads of sweat. He was gasping slightly through his open mouth, and his hands were restlessly pulling at the blanket which covered him. He was still wearing his green-and-red-checked racing colours, the most ominous sign of all.

Scilla said to me, 'I'm going with him in the ambulance. Can you come?'

'I've a ride in the last race,' I said. 'I'll come along to the hospital straight after that. Don't worry, he'll be all right.' But I didn't believe it, and nor did she.

After they had gone I walked along beside the weighing-room building and down through the car park until I came to the bank of the river. Swollen from recently melted snow, the Thames was flowing fast, sandy-brown and grey with froths of white. The water swirled out of the mist a hundred yards to my right, churned round the bend where I stood and disappeared again into the fog. Troubled, confused, not seeing a clear course ahead. Just like me.

For there was something wrong about Bill's accident.

Back in Bulawayo, where I got my schooling, the mathematics master spent hours (too many, I thought in my youth) teaching us to draw correct inferences from a few known facts. But deduction was his hobby as well as his job, and occasionally we had been able to side-track him from problems of geometry or algebra to those of Sherlock Holmes. He produced class after class of boys keenly observant of well-worn toe-caps on char-women and vicars and calluses on the finger tips of harpists; and the mathematics standard of the school was exceptionally high.

Now, thousands of miles and seven years away from the sun-baked schoolroom, standing in an English fog and growing very cold, I remembered my master and took out my facts, and had a look at them.

Known facts ... Admiral, a superb jumper, had fallen abruptly in full flight for no apparent reason. The racecourse attendant had walked across the course behind the fence as Bill and I rode towards it, but this was not at all unusual. And as I had cleared the fence, and while I was looking down at Bill, somewhere on the edge of my vision there had been a dull, damp gleam from something grey and metallic. I thought about these things for a long time.

The inference was there all right, but unbelievable. I had to find out if it was the correct one.

I went back into the weighing room to collect my kit and weigh out for the last race, but as I packed the flat lead pieces into my weight cloth to bring my weight up to that set by the handicapper, the loudspeakers were turned on and it was announced that, owing to the thickening fog, the last race had been abandoned.

There was a rush then in the changing room, and the tea and fruit-cake disappeared at a quickened tempo. It was a long time since breakfast, and I stuffed a couple of beef sandwiches into my mouth while I changed. I arranged with Clem for my kit to go to Plumpton, where I was due to ride four days later, and set off on an uninviting walk. I wanted to have a close look at the place where Bill had fallen.

It is a long way on foot from the stands to the far end of Maidenhead racecourse, and by the time I got there my shoes, socks and trouser legs were wet through from the long, sodden grass. It was very cold, very foggy. There was no one about.

I reached the fence, the harmless, softish, easy-to-jump fence, made of black birch twigs standing upright. Three feet thick at the bottom slanting to half that size at the top, four feet six inches tall, about ten yards wide. Ordinary, easy.

I looked carefully along the landing side of the fence. There was nothing unusual. Round I went to the take-off side. Nothing. I poked around the wing which guides the horses into the fence, the one on the inside of the course, the side Bill had been when he fell. Still nothing.

It was down underneath the wing on the outside of the course that I found what I was looking for. There it lay in the long grass, half hidden, beaded with drops of mist, coiled and deadly.

Wire.

There was a good deal of it, a pale silver-grey, wound into a ring about a foot across and weighted down with a piece of wood. One end of it led up the main side post of the wing and was fastened round it two feet above the level of the top of the birch. Fastened, I saw, very securely indeed. I could not untwist it with my fingers.

I went back to the inside wing and had a look at the post. Two feet above the fence there was a groove in the wood. This post had once been painted white, and the mark showed clearly.

It was clear to me that only one person could have fixed the wire in place. The attendant. The man whom I myself had seen walk across from one side of the course to the other. The man, I thought bitterly, whom I had left to *help* Bill.

In a three-mile 'chase at Maidenhead one rode twice round the course. On the first circuit there had been no trouble at this fence. Nine horses had jumped it safely, with Admiral lying third and biding his time, and me riding alongside telling Bill I didn't think much of the English climate.

Second time round, Admiral was lengths out in front. As soon as the attendant had seen him land over the fence before this one, he must have walked over, holding the free end of wire, and wound it round the opposite post so that it stretched there taut in the air, almost invisible, two feet above the birch. At that height it would catch the high-leaping Admiral straight across the shoulders.

The callousness of it awoke a slow deep anger which, though I did not then know it, was to remain with me as a spur for many weeks to come.

Whether the horse had snapped the wire when he hit it, or pulled it off the post, I could not be sure. But as I could find no separate pieces, and the coil by the outer wing was all one length, I thought it likely that the falling horse had jerked the less secure end down with him. None of the seven horses following me had been brought down. Like me, they must have jumped clear over the remains of the trap.

Unless the attendant was a lunatic, which could by no means be ruled out, it was a deliberate attack on a particular horse and rider. Bill on Admiral had normally reached the front by this stage in a race, often having opened up a lead of twenty lengths, and his red and green colours, even on a misty day, were easy to see.

At this point, greatly disturbed, I began the walk back. It was already growing dark. I had been longer at the fence than I had realized, and when I at length reached the weighing room, intending to tell the Clerk of the Course about the wire, I found everyone except the caretaker had gone.

The caretaker, who was old and bad-tempered and incessantly sucked his teeth, told me he did not know where the Clerk of the Course could be found. He said the racecourse manager had driven off towards the town five minutes earlier. He did not know where the manager had been going, nor when he would be back; and with a grumbling tale that he had five separate stoves besides the central boiler to see to, and that the fog was bad for his bronchitis, the caretaker shuffled purposefully off towards the dim murky bulk of the grandstand.

Undecided, I watched him go. I ought, I knew, to tell someone in authority about the wire. But who? The Stewards who had been at the meeting were all on their way home, creeping wearily through the fog, unreachable. The manager had gone; the Clerk of the Course's office, I discovered, was locked. It would take me a long time to locate any of them, persuade them to return to the racecourse and get them to drive down the course over the rough ground in the dark; and after that there would be discussion, repetition, statements. It would be hours before I could get away.

Meanwhile Bill was fighting for his life in

Maidenhead hospital, and I wanted profoundly to know if he were winning. Scilla faced racking hours of anxiety and I had promised to be with her as soon as I could. Already I had delayed too long. The wire, fogbound and firmly twisted round the post, would keep until tomorrow, I thought; but Bill might not.

Bill's Jaguar was alone in the car park. I climbed in, switched on the side lights and the fog lights and drove off. I turned left at the gates, went gingerly along the road for two miles, turned left again over the river, twisted through Maidenhead's one-way streets, and finally arrived at the hospital.

There was no sign of Scilla in the brightly lit busy hall. I asked the porter.

'Mrs Davidson? Husband a jockey? That's right, she's down there in the waiting room. Fourth door on the left.'

I found her. Her dark eyes looked enormous, shadowed with grey smudges beneath them. All other colour had gone from her sad strained face, and she had taken off her frivolous hat.

'How is he?' I asked.

'I don't know. They just tell me not to worry.'

 She was very close to tears.

I sat down beside her and held her hand.

'You're a comfort, Alan,' she said.

Presently the door opened and a fair young doctor came in, stethoscope dangling.

'Mrs Davidson, I think . . .' he paused, 'I think you should come and sit with your husband.'

'How is he?'

'Not . . . very well. We are doing all we can.' Turning to me he said, 'Are you a relative?'

'A friend. I am going to drive Mrs Davidson home.'

'I see,' he said. 'Will you wait or come back for her? Later this evening.' There was meaning in his careful voice, his neutral words. I looked closely into his face, and I knew that Bill was dying.

'I'll wait.'

'Good.'

I waited for four hours, getting to know intimately the pattern of the curtains and the cracks in the brown linoleum. Mostly, I thought about wire.

At last a nurse came, serious, young, pretty.

'I am so sorry . . . Major Davidson is dead.'

Mrs Davidson would like me to go and see him,

she said, if I would follow her. She took me down the long corridors, and into a white room, not very big, where Scilla sat beside the single bed.

Scilla looked up at me. She couldn't speak.

Bill lay there, grey and quiet, finished. The best friend a man could wish for.

The Gift

When the breakfast-time Astrojet from La Guardia was still twenty minutes short of Louisville, Fred Collyer took out a block of printed forms and began to write his expenses.

Cab fare to airport, fifteen dollars.

No matter that a neighbour, working out on Long Island, had given a free ride door to door: a little imagination in the expense department earned him half as much again (untaxed) as the *Manhattan Star* paid him for the facts he came up with every week in his Monday racing column.

Refreshments on journey, he wrote, *five dollars.*

Entertaining for the purposes of obtaining information, six dollars fifty.

To justify that little lot he ordered a second double Bourbon from the air hostess and lifted it in a silent good-luck gesture to a man sleeping across the aisle, the owner of a third-rate filly that had bucked her shins two weeks ago.

Another Kentucky Derby. His mind flickered

like a scratched print of an old movie over the days ahead. The same old slog out to the barns in the mornings, the same endless raking over of past form, searching for a hint of the future. The same inconclusive work-outs on the track, the same slanderous rumours, the same gossip, the same stupid jocks, the same stupid trainers, shooting their goddam stupid mouths off.

The bright-burning enthusiasm which had carved out his syndicated by-line was long gone. The lift of the spirit to the big occasion, the flair for sensing a story when no one else did, the sharp instinct which sorted truth from camouflage, all these he had had. All had left him. In their place lay plains of boredom and perpetual cynical tiredness. Instead of exclusives he nowadays gave his paper rehashes of other turfwriters' ideas, and a couple of times recently he had failed to do even that.

He was forty-six.

He drank.

Back in his functional New York office the Sports Editor of the *Manhattan Star* pursed his lips over Fred Collyer's account of the Everglades at Hialeah and wondered if he had been wise to send him down as usual to the Derby.

That guy, he thought regretfully, was all washed up. Too bad. Too bad he couldn't stay off the liquor. No one could drink and write, not at one and the same time. Write first, drink after, sure. Drink to excess, to stupor, maybe. But *after*.

He thought that before long he would have to let Fred go, that probably he should have started looking around for a replacement that day months back when Fred first turned up in the office too fuddled to hit the right keys on his typewriter. But that bum had had everything, he thought. A true journalist's nose for a story, and a gift for putting it across so vividly that the words jumped right off the page and kicked you in the brain.

Nowadays all that was left was a reputation and an echo: the technique still marched shakily on, but the personality behind it was drowning.

The Sports Editor shook his head over the Hialeah clipping and laid it aside. Twice in the past six weeks Fred had been incapable of writing a story at all. Each time when he had not phoned through they had fudged up a column in the office and stuck the Collyer name on it, but two missed deadlines were one more than forgivable. Three, and it would be all over. The management were grumbling louder than ever over the inflated expense accounts, and if they found out that in return they had twice received only sodden silence, no amount of for-old-times' sake would save him.

I did warn him, thought the Sports Editor uneasily. I told him to be sure to turn in a good one this time. A sizzler, like he used to. I told him to make this Derby one of his greats.

Fred Collyer checked into the motel room the newspaper had reserved for him and sank three quick mid-morning stiffeners from the bottle he had brought along in his briefcase. He shoved the Sports Editor's warning to the back of his mind because he was still sure that, drunk or sober, he could outwrite any other commentator in the business, given a story that was worth the trouble. There just weren't any good stories around any more.

He took a taxi out to Churchill Downs. (*Cab fare, four dollars fifty*, he wrote on the way; and paid the driver two seventy-five.)

With three days to go to the Derby the racecourse looked clean, fresh and expectant. Bright-red tulips in tidy columns pointed their petals uniformly to the blue sky, and patches of green grass glowed like shampooed rugs. Without noticing them Fred Collyer took the elevator to the roof and trudged up the last windy steps to the huge glass-fronted press room which ran along the top of the stands. Inside, a few men sat at the rows of typewriters knocking out the next day's news, and a few more stood outside on the balcony actually watching the first race, but most were engaged on the day's serious business, which was chat.

Fred Collyer bought himself a can of beer at the simple bar and carried it over to his named place, exchanging hi-yahs with the faces he saw on the circuit from Saratoga to Hollywood Park. Living on the move in hotels, and altogether rootless since Sylvie got fed up with his absence and his drinking and took the kids back to Mom in Nebraska, he looked upon racecourse press rooms as his only real home. He felt relaxed there, assured of respect. He was unaware that the admiration he had once inspired was slowly fading into tolerant pity.

He sat easily in his chair reading one of the day's duplicated news releases.

'Trainer Harbourne Cressie reports no heat in Pincer Movement's near fore after breezing four furlongs on the track this morning.'

'No truth in rumour that Salad Bowl was running a temperature last evening, insists veterinarian John Brewer on behalf of owner Mrs L. (Loretta) Hicks.'

Marvellous, he thought sarcastically. Negative news was no news, Derby runners included.

He stayed up in the press room all afternoon, drinking beer, discussing this, that and nothing with writers, photographers, publicists and radio newsmen, keeping an inattentive eye on the racing on the closed-circuit television, and occasionally going out onto the balcony to look down on the anthill crowd far beneath. There was no need to struggle around down there as he used to, he thought. No need to try to see people, to interview them privately. Everything and everyone of interest came up to the press room sometime, ladling out info in spoonfed dollops.

At the end of the day he accepted a ride back to town in a colleague's Hertz car (*cab fare, four dollars fifty*) and in the evening having laid substantial Bourbon foundations in his own room before setting out he attended the annual dinner of the Turfwriters' Association. The throng in the big reception room was pleased enough to see him, and he moved among the assortment of pressmen, trainers, jockeys, breeders, owners and wives and girlfriends like a fish in his own home pond. Automatically before dinner he put away four doubles on the rocks, and through the food and the lengthy speeches afterwards kept up a steady intake. At half after eleven, when he tried to leave the table, he couldn't control his legs.

It surprised him. Sitting down, he had not been aware of being drunk. His tongue still worked as well as most around him, and to himself his thoughts seemed perfectly well organized. But his legs buckled as he put his weight on them, and he returned to his seat with a thump. It was considerably later, when the huge room had almost emptied as the guests went home, that he managed to summon enough strength to stand up.

'Guess I took a skinful,' he murmured, smiling to himself in self-excuse.

Holding on to the backs of chairs and at intervals leaning against the wall, he weaved his way to the door. From there he blundered out into the passage and forward to the lobby, and from there, looking as if he were climbing imaginary steps, out into the night through the swinging glass doors.

The cool May evening air made things much worse. The earth seemed literally to be turning beneath his feet. He listed sideways into a half circle and instead of moving forwards towards the parked cars and waiting taxis, staggered head-on into the dark brick front of the wall flanking the entrance. The impact hurt him and confused him further. He put both his hands flat on the rough surface in front of him and laid his face on it, and couldn't work out where he was.

Marius Tollman and Piper Boles had not seen Fred Collyer leave ahead of them. They strolled together along the same route making the ordinary social phrases and gestures of people who had just come together by chance at the end of an evening, and gave no impression at all that they had been eyeing each other meaningfully across the room for hours, and thinking almost exclusively about the conversation which lay ahead.

 In a country with legalized bookmaking Marius

Tollman might have grown up a respectable law-abiding citizen. As it was, his natural aptitude and only talent had led him into a lifetime of quick footwork which would have done credit to Muhammad Ali. Through the simple expedient of standing bets for the future racing authorities while they were still young enough to be foolish, he remained unpersecuted by them once they reached status and power; and the one sort of winner old crafty Marius could spot better even than horses was the colt heading for the boardroom.

The two men went through the glass doors and stopped just outside with the light from the lobby shining full upon them. Marius never drew people into corners, believing it looked too suspicious.

'Did you get the boys to go along, then?' he asked, standing on his heels with his hands in his pockets and his paunch oozing over his belt.

Piper Boles slowly lit a cigarette, glanced around casually at the star dotted sky, and sucked comforting smoke into his lungs.

'Yeah,' he said.

'So who's elected?'

'Amberezzio.'

'No,' Marius protested. 'He's not good enough.'

Piper Boles drew deep on his cigarette. He was hungry. One eleven pounds to make tomorrow, and only a five ounce steak in his belly. He resented fat people, particularly rich fat people. He was putting away his own small store of fat in real estate and growth bonds, but at thirty-eight the physical struggle was near to defeating him. He couldn't face many more years of starvation, finding it worse as his body aged. A sense of urgency had lately led him to consider ways of making a quick ten thousand that once he would have sneered at.

He said, 'He's straight. It'll have to be him.'

Marius thought it over, not liking it, but finally nodded.

'All right, then. Amberezzio.'

Piper Boles nodded, and prepared to move away. It didn't do for a jockey to be seen too long with Marius Tollman, not if he wanted to go on riding second string for the prestigious Somerset Farms, which he most assuredly did.

 Marius saw the impulse and said smoothly,

'Did you give any thought to a diversion on Crinkle Cut?'

Piper Boles hesitated.

'It'll cost you,' he said.

'Sure,' Marius agreed easily. 'How about another thousand, on top?'

'Used bills. Half before.'

'Sure.'

Piper Boles shrugged off his conscience, tossed out the last of his integrity.

'OK,' he said, and sauntered away to his car as if all his nerves weren't stretched and screaming.

Fred Collyer had heard every word, and he knew, without having to look, that one of the voices was Marius Tollman's. Impossible for anyone long in the racing game not to recognize the wheezy Boston accent. He understood that Marius had been fixing up a swindle and also that a good little swindle would fill his column nicely. He thought fuzzily that it was necessary to know who Marius had been talking to, and that as the voices had been behind him he had better turn round and find out.

Time however was disjointed for him, and when

he pushed himself off the wall and made an effort to focus in the right direction, both men had gone.

'Bastards,' he said aloud to the empty night, and another late homegoer, leaving the hotel, took him compassionately by the elbow and led him to a taxi. He made it safely back to his own room before he passed out.

Since leaving La Guardia that morning he had drunk six beers, four brandies, one double Scotch (by mistake), and nearly three fifths of Bourbon.

He woke at eleven the next morning, and couldn't believe it. He stared at the bedside clock.

Eleven.

He had missed the barns and the whole morning merry-go-round on the track. A shiver chilled him at that first realization, but there was worse to come. When he tried to sit up the room whirled and his head thumped like a pile driver. When he stripped back the sheet he found he had been sleeping in bed fully clothed with his shoes on. When he tried to remember how he had returned the previous evening, he could not do so.

He tottered into the bathroom. His face looked back at him like a nightmare from the mirror, wrinkled and red-eyed, ten years older overnight. Hungover he had been any number of times, but this felt like no ordinary morning-after. A sense of irretrievable disaster hovered somewhere behind the acute physical misery of his head and stomach, but it was not until he had taken off his coat and shirt and pants, and scraped off his shoes, and lain down again weakly on the crumpled bed, that he discovered its nature.

Then he realized with a jolt that not only had he no recollection of the journey back to his motel, he could recall practically nothing of the entire evening. Snatches of conversation from the first hour came back to him, and he remembered sitting at table between a cross old writer from the *Baltimore Sun* and an earnest woman breeder from Lexington, neither of whom he liked; but an uninterrupted blank started from half-way through the fried chicken.

He had heard of alcoholic blackouts, but supposed they only happened to alcoholics; and he, Fred Collyer, was not one of those. Of course, he would concede that he did drink a little. Well, a lot, then. But he could stop any time he liked. Naturally he could.

He lay on the bed and sweated, facing the stark thought that one blackout might lead to another, until blackouts gave way to pink panthers climbing the walls. The Sports Editor's warning came back with a bang, and for the first time, uncomfortably remembering the twice he had missed his column, he felt a shade of anxiety about his job. Within five minutes he had reassured himself that they would never fire Fred Collyer, but all the same he would for the paper's sake lay off the drink until after he had written his piece on the Derby. This resolve gave him a glowing feeling of selfless virtue, which at least helped him through the shivering fits and pulsating headaches of an extremely wretched day.

Out at Churchill Downs three other men were just as worried. Piper Boles kicked his horse forward into the starting stalls and worried about what George Highbury, the Somerset Farms trainer, had said when he went to scale at two pounds overweight. George Highbury thought himself superior to all jocks and spoke to them curtly, win or lose.

'Don't give me that crap,' he said to Boles' excuses. 'You went to the Turfwriters' dinner last night, what do you expect?'

Piper Boles looked bleakly back over his hungry evening with its single martini and said he'd had a session in the sweat box that morning.

Highbury scowled. 'You keep your fat ass away from the table tonight and tomorrow if you want to make Crinkle Cut in the Derby.'

Piper Boles badly needed to ride Crinkle Cut in the Derby. He nodded meekly to Highbury with downcast eyes, and swung unhappily into the saddle.

Instead of bracing him, the threat of losing the ride on Crinkle Cut took the edge off his concentration, so that he came out of the stalls slowly, streaked the first quarter too fast to reach third place, swung wide at the bend and lost his stride straightening out. He finished sixth. He was a totally experienced jockey of above average ability. It was not one of his days.

On the grandstand Marius Tollman put down his raceglasses shaking his head and clicking his tongue. If Piper Boles couldn't ride a better race than that when he was supposed to be trying to win, what sort of a goddam hash would he make of losing on Crinkle Cut?

Marius thought about the ten thousand he was staking on Saturday's little caper. He had not yet decided whether to tip off certain guys in organized crime, in which case they would cover the stake at no risk to himself, or to gamble on the bigger profit of going it alone. He lowered his wheezy bulk on to his seat and worried about the ease with which a fixed race could unfix itself.

Blisters Schultz worried about the state of his trade, which was suffering a severe recession.

Blisters Schultz picked pockets for a living, and was fed up with credit cards. In the old days, when he'd learned the skill at his grandfather's knee, men carried their billfolds in their rear pants' pockets, neatly outlined for all the world to see. Nowadays all these smash and grab muggers had ruined the market: few people carried more than a handful of dollars around with them, and those that did tended to divide it into two portions, with the heavy dough hidden away beneath zips.

Fifty-three years Blisters had survived: forty-five of them by stealing. Several shortish sessions behind bars had been regarded as bad luck, but not as a good reason for not nicking the first wallet he saw when he got out. He had tried to go straight once, but he hadn't liked it: couldn't face the regular hours and the awful feeling of working. After six weeks he had left his well-paid job and gone back thankfully to insecurity. He felt happier stealing two dollars than earning ten.

For the best haul at racemeets you either had to spot the big wads before they were gambled away, or follow a big winner away from the pay-out window. In either case, it meant hanging around the pari-mutuel with your eyes open. The trouble was, too many racecourse cops had cottoned to this modus op, and were apt to stand around looking at people who were just standing there looking.

Blisters had had a bad week. The most promisingly fat wallet had proved, after half an hour's careful stalking, to contain little money but a lot of pornography. Blisters, having a weak sex drive, was disgusted on both counts.

For his first two days' labour he had only

twenty-three dollars to show, and five of these he had found on a stairway. His meagre room in Louisville was costing him eight a night, and with transport and eating to take into account, he reckoned he'd have to clear three hundred to make the trip worth while.

Always an optimist, he brightened at the thought of Derby Day. The pickings would certainly be easier once the real crowd arrived.

Fred Collyer's private Prohibition lasted intact through Friday. Feeling better when he awoke, he cabbed out to Churchill Downs at seven thirty, writing his expenses on the way. They included many mythical items for the previous day, on the basis that it was better for the office not to know he had been paralytic on Wednesday night. He upped the inflated total a few more dollars: after all, Bourbon was expensive, and he would be off the wagon by Sunday.

The initial shock of the blackout had worn off, because during his day in bed he had remembered bits and pieces which he was certain were later in time than the fried chicken. The journey from
 dinner to bed was still a blank, but the blank had

stopped frightening him. At times he felt there was something vital about it he ought to remember, but he persuaded himself that if it had been really important, he wouldn't have forgotten.

Out by the barns the groups of pressmen had already formed round the trainers of the most fancied Derby runners. Fred Collyer sauntered to the outskirts of Harbourne Cressie, and his colleagues made room for him with no reference to his previous day's absence. It reassured him: whatever he had done on Wednesday night, it couldn't have been scandalous.

The notebooks were out. Harbourne Cressie, long-practised and fond of publicity, paused between every sentence to give time for all to be written down.

'Pincer Movement ate well last evening and is calm and cool this a.m. On the book we should hold Salad Bowl, unless the track is sloppy by Saturday.'

Smiles all round. The sky blue, the forecast fair.

Fred Collyer listened without attention. He'd heard it all before. They'd all heard it all before. And who the hell cared?

In a rival group two barns away the trainer of Salad Bowl was saying his colt had the beating of Pincer Movement on the Hialeah form and could run on any going, sloppy or not.

George Highbury attracted fewer newsmen, as he hadn't much to say about Crinkle Cut. The three-year-old had been beaten by both Pincer Movement and Salad Bowl on separate occasions and was not expected to reverse things.

On Friday afternoon Fred Collyer spent his time up in the press room and manfully refused a couple of free beers. (*Entertaining various owners at track, twenty-two dollars.*)

Piper Boles rode a hard finish in the sixth race, lost by a short head and almost passed out from hunger-induced weakness in the jocks' room afterwards. George Highbury, unaware of this, merely noted sourly that Boles had made the weight and confirmed that he would ride Crinkle Cut on the morrow.

Various friends of Piper Boles, supporting him towards a daybed, asked anxiously in his ear whether tomorrow's scheme was still on. Piper Boles nodded. 'Sure,' he said faintly. 'All the way.'

Marius Tollman was relieved to see Boles riding better but decided anyway to hedge his bet by letting the syndicate in on the action.

Blisters Schultz lifted two billfolds, containing respectively fourteen and twenty-two dollars. He lost ten of them backing a certainty in the last race.

Pincer Movement, Salad Bowl and Crinkle Cut, guarded by uniformed men with guns at their waists, looked over the stable doors and with small quivers in their tuned-up muscles watched other horses go out to the track. All three would have chosen to go too. All three knew well enough what the trumpet was sounding for, on the other side.

Saturday morning, fine and clear.

Crowds in their thousands converged on Churchill Downs. Eager, expectant, chattering, dressed in bright colours and buying mint juleps in takeaway souvenir glasses, they poured through the gates and over the infield, reading the latest sports columns on Pincer Movement versus Salad Bowl and dreaming of picking outsiders that came up at fifty to one.

Blisters Schultz had scraped together just enough to pay his motel bill, but self-esteem depended on better luck with the hoists. His small, lined face with its busy eyes wore a look near to desperation, and the long predatory fingers clenched and unclenched convulsively in his pockets.

Piper Boles, with one-twenty-six to do on Crinkle Cut, allowed himself an egg for breakfast and decided to buy property bonds with the five hundred in used notes which had been delivered by hand the previous evening and with the gains (both legal and illegal) he should add to them that day. If he cleaned up safely that afternoon, he thought, there was no obvious reason why he shouldn't set up the same scheme again, even after he had retired from riding. He hardly noticed the shift in his mind from reluctant dishonesty to habitual fraud.

Marius Tollman spent the morning telephoning to various acquaintances, offering profit. His offers were accepted. Marius Tollman felt a load lift from his spirits and with a spring in his step took his two-sixty pounds downtown a few blocks, where a careful gentleman counted out ten thou-

 sand dollars in untraceable notes. Marius Tollman

gave him a receipt, properly signed. Business was business.

Fred Collyer wanted a drink. One, he thought, wouldn't hurt. It would pep him up a bit, put him on his toes. One little drink in the morning would certainly not stop him writing a punchy piece that evening. The *Star* couldn't possibly frown on just *one* drink before he went to the races, especially not as he had managed to keep clear of the bar the previous evening by going to bed at nine. His abstinence had involved a great effort of will: it would be right to reward such virtue with just one drink.

He had, however, finished on Wednesday night the bottle he had brought with him to Louisville. He fished out his wallet to check how much he had in it: fifty-three dollars, plenty after expenses to cover a fresh bottle for later as well as a quick one in the bar before he left.

He went downstairs. In the lobby, however, his colleague Clay Petrovitch again offered a free ride in his Hertz car to Churchill Downs, so he decided he could postpone his one drink for half an hour. He gave himself little mental pats on the back all the way to the racecourse.

Blisters Schultz, circulating among the clusters of people at the rear of the grandstand, saw Marius Tollman going by in the sunshine, leaning backwards to support the weight in front and wheezing audibly in the growing heat.

Blisters Schultz licked his lips. He knew the fat man by sight: knew that somewhere around that gross body might be stacked enough lolly to see him through the summer. Marius Tollman would never come to the Derby with empty pockets.

Two thoughts made Blisters hesitate as he slid like an eel in the fat man's wake. The first was that Tollman was too old a hand to let himself be robbed. The second, that he was known to have friends in organized places, and if Tollman was carrying organization money Blisters wasn't going to burn his fingers by stealing it, which was how he got his nickname in the first place.

Regretfully Blisters peeled off from the quarry and returned to the throng in the comforting shadows under the grandstand.

At twelve-seventeen he infiltrated a close-packed bunch of people waiting for an elevator.

At twelve-eighteen he stole Fred Collyer's wallet.

Marius Tollman carried his money in cunning underarm pockets which he clamped to his sides in a crowd, for fear of pickpockets. When the time was due he would visit as many different selling windows as possible, inconspicuously distributing the stake. He would give Piper Boles almost half of the tickets (along with the second five hundred dollars in used notes) and keep the other half for himself.

A nice tidy little killing, he thought complacently. And no reason why he shouldn't set it up some time again.

He bought a mint julep and smiled kindly at a girl showing more bosom than bashfulness.

The sun stoked up the day. The preliminary contests rolled over one by one with waves of cheering, each hard-ridden finish merely a sideshow attending on the big one, the Derby, the roses, the climax, the ninth race.

In the jocks' room Piper Boles had changed into the silks for Crinkle Cut and began to sweat. The nearer he came to the race the more he wished it was an ordinary Derby day like any other. He steadied his nerves by reading the *Financial Times*.

Fred Collyer discovered the loss of his wallet

upstairs in the press room when he tried to pay for a beer. He cursed, searched all his pockets, turned the press room upside down, got the keys of the Hertz car from Clay Petrovitch and trailed all the way back to the car park. After a fruitless search there he strode furiously back to the grandstands, violently throttling in his mind the lousy stinking son of a bitch who had stolen his money. He guessed it had been an old hand, an old man, even. The new vicious young lot relied on muscle, not skill.

His practical problems were not too great. He needed little cash. Clay Petrovitch was taking him back to town, the motel bill was going direct to the *Manhattan Star* and his plane ticket was safely lying in the chest of drawers in his bedroom. He could borrow twenty bucks or so, maybe, from Clay or others in the press room to cover essentials.

Going up in the elevator he thought that the loss of his money was like a sign from heaven; no money, no drink.

Blisters Schultz kept Fred Collyer sober the whole afternoon.

Pincer Movement, Salad Bowl and Crinkle Cut were led from their barns, into the tunnel under the cars and crowd and out again on to the track in front of the grandstands. They walked loosely, casually, used to the limelight but knowing from experience that this was only a foretaste. The first sight of the day's princes galvanized the crowds towards the pari-mutuel window like shoals of multi-coloured fish.

Piper Boles walked out with the other jockeys towards the wire-meshed enclosure where horses, trainers and owners stood in a group in each stall. He had begun to suffer from a feeling of detachment and unreality: he could not believe that he, a basically honest jockey, was about to make a hash of the Kentucky Derby.

George Highbury repeated for about the fortieth time the tactics they had agreed on. Piper Boles nodded seriously, as if he had every intention of carrying them out. He actually heard scarcely a word; and he was deaf also to the massed bands and the singing when the Derby runners were led out to the track. 'My Old Kentucky Home' swelled the emotions of a multitude and brought out a flutter of eye-wiping handkerchiefs, but in Piper Boles they raised not a blink.

Through the parade, the canter down, the circling round, and even into the starting stalls, the detachment persisted. Only then, with the tension showing plain on the faces of the other riders, did he click back to realization. His heart-rate nearly doubled and energy flooded into his brain.

Now, he thought. It is now, in the next half minute, that I earn myself one thousand dollars; and after that, the rest.

He pulled down his goggles and gathered his reins and his whip. He had Pincer Movement on his right and Salad Bowl on his left, and when the stalls sprang open he went out between them in a rush, tipping his weight instantly forward over the withers and standing in the stirrups with his head almost as far forward as Crinkle Cut's.

All along past the stands the first time he concentrated on staying in the centre of the main bunch, as unnoticeable as possible, and round the top bend he was still there, sitting quietly and doing nothing very much. But down the backstretch, lying about tenth in a field of twenty-six, he earned his thousand.

No one except Piper Boles ever knew what really happened; only he knew that he'd shortened his left rein with a sharp turn of his wrist and squeezed Crinkle Cut's ribs with his right foot. The fast-galloping horse obeyed these directions, veered abruptly left and crashed into the horse beside him.

The horse beside him was still Salad Bowl. Under the impact Salad Bowl cannoned into the horse on his own left, rocked back, stumbled, lost his footing entirely and fell. The two horses on his tail fell over him.

Piper Boles didn't look back. The swerve and collision had lost him several places which Crinkle Cut at the best of times would have been unable to make up. He rode the rest of the race strictly according to his instructions, finishing flat out in twelfth place.

Of the one hundred and forty thousand spectators at Churchill Downs, only a handful had had a clear view of the disaster on the far side of the track. The buildings in the infield, and the milling crowds filling all its furthest areas, had hidden the crash from nearly all standing at ground level and from most on the grandstands. Only the press, high up, had seen. They sent out urgent fact-finders and buzzed like a stirred up beehive.

Fred Collyer, out on the balcony, watched the photographers running to immortalize Pincer Movement and reflected sourly that none of them would have taken close-up pictures of the second favourite, Salad Bowl, down on the dirt. He watched the horseshoe of dark-red roses being draped over the winner and the triumphal presentation of the trophies, and then went inside for the re-run of the race on television. They showed the Salad Bowl incident forwards, backwards and sideways, and then jerked it through slowly in a series of stills.

'See that,' said Clay Petrovitch, pointing at the screen over Fred Collyer's shoulder. 'It was Crinkle Cut caused it. You can see him crash into Salad Bowl . . . there! . . . Crinkle Cut, that's the joker in the pack.'

Fred Collyer strolled over to his place, sat down, and stared at his typewriter. Crinkle Cut. He knew something about Crinkle Cut. He thought intensely for five minutes, but couldn't remember what he knew.

Details and quotes came up to the press room. All fallen jocks shaken but unhurt, all horses ditto; stewards in a tizzy, making instant inquiries and re-running the patrol camera film over and over. Suspension for Piper Boles considered unlikely, as blind eye usually turned to rough riding in the Derby. Piper Boles had gone on record as saying, 'Crinkle Cut just suddenly swerved. I didn't expect it, and couldn't prevent him bumping Salad Bowl.' Large numbers of people believed him.

Fred Collyer thought he might as well get a few pars down on paper: it would bring the first drink nearer and, boy, how he needed that drink. With an ear open for fresher information he tapped out a blow-by-blow I-was-there account of an incident he had hardly seen. When he began to read it through, he saw the first words he had written were 'The diversion on Crinkle Cut stole the post-race scene . . .'

Diversion on Crinkle Cut? He hadn't meant to write that . . . or not exactly. He frowned. And there were other words in his mind, just as stupid. He put his hands back on the keys and tapped them out.

'It'll cost you . . . a thousand in used notes . . . half before.'

He stared at what he had written. He had made

it up, he must have. Or dreamed it. One or the other.

A dream. That was it. He remembered. He had had a dream about two men planning a fixed race, and one of them had been Marius Tollman, wheezing away about a diversion on Crinkle Cut.

Fred Collyer relaxed and smiled at the thought, and the next minute knew quite suddenly that it hadn't been a dream at all. He had heard Marius Tollman and Piper Boles planning a diversion on Crinkle Cut, and he had forgotten because he'd been drunk. Well, he reassured himself uneasily, no harm done, he had remembered now, hadn't he?

No, he hadn't. If Crinkle Cut was a diversion, what was he a diversion *from*? Perhaps if he waited a bit, he would find he knew that too.

Blisters Schultz spent Fred Collyer's money on two hot dogs, one mint julep and five losing bets. On the winning side, he had harvested three more billfolds and a woman's purse: total haul, ninety-four bucks. Gloomily he decided to call it a day and not come back next year.

Marius Tollman lumbered busily from window

to window of the pari-mutuel and the stewards asked to see the jockeys involved in the Salad Bowl pile-up.

The crowds, hot, tired and frayed at the edges, began to leave in the yellowing sunshine. The bands marched away. The stalls which sold souvenirs packed up their wares. Pincer Movement had his picture taken for the thousandth time, and the runners for the tenth, last and least interesting race of the day walked over from the barns.

Piper Boles was waiting outside the stewards' room for a summons inside, but Marius Tollman used the highest-class messengers, and the package he entrusted was safely delivered. Piper Boles nodded, slipped it into his pocket and gave the stewards a performance worthy of Hollywood.

Fred Collyer put his head in his hands, trying to remember. A drink, he thought, might help. Diversion. Crinkle Cut. Amberezzio.

He sat up sharply. *Amberezzio.* And what the hell did that mean? *It has to be Amberezzio.*

'Clay,' he said, leaning back over his chair. 'Do you know of a horse called Amberezzio?'

Clay Petrovitch shook his bald head. 'Never heard of it.'

Fred Collyer called to several others through the hubbub, 'Know of a horse called Amberezzio?' And finally he got an answer. 'Amberezzio isn't a horse, he's an apprentice.'

'*It has to be Amberezzio. He's straight.*'

Fred Collyer knocked his chair over as he stood up. They had already called one minute to post time on the last race.

'Lend me twenty bucks, there's a pal,' he said to Clay.

Clay, knowing about the lost wallet, amiably agreed and slowly began to bring out his money.

'Hurry, for Chrissake,' Fred Collyer said urgently.

'OK, OK.' He handed over the twenty dollars and turned back to his own typewriter.

Fred Collyer grabbed his racecard and pushed through the post-Derby chatter to the pari-mutuel window further along the press floor. He flipped the pages . . . Tenth race, Homeward Bound, claiming race, eight runners . . . His eye skimmed down the list, and found what he sought.

Phillip Amberezzio, riding a horse Fred Collyer had never heard of.

'Twenty on the nose, number six,' he said quickly, and received his ticket seconds before the window was shut. Trembling slightly, he pushed back through the crowd, and out on to the balcony. He was the only pressman watching the race.

Those jocks did it beautifully, he thought in admiration. Artistic. You wouldn't have known if you hadn't known. They bunched him in and shepherded him along, and then at the perfect moment gave him a suddenly clear opening. Amberezzio won by half a length, with all the others waving their whips as if beating the last inch out of their mounts.

Fred Collyer laughed. That poor little so-and-so probably thought he was a hell of a fellow, bringing home a complete outsider with all the big boys baying at his heels.

He went back inside the press room and found everyone's attention directed towards Harbourne Cressie, who had brought with him the owner and jockey of Pincer Movement. Fred Collyer dutifully took down enough quotes to cover the subject, but his mind was on the other story, the big one, the gift.

It would need careful handling, he thought. It would need the very best he could do, as he would have to be careful not to make direct accusations while leaving it perfectly clear that an investigation was necessary. His old instincts partially re-awoke. He was even excited. He would write his piece in the quiet and privacy of his own room in the motel. Couldn't do it here on the racecourse, with every turfwriter in the world looking over his shoulder.

Down in the jockeys' changing room Piper Boles quietly distributed the pari-mutuel tickets which Marius Tollman had delivered: five hundred dollars' worth to each of the seven 'unsuccessful' riders in the tenth race, and one thousand dollars' worth to himself. Each jockey subsequently asked a wife or girlfriend to collect the winnings and several of these would have made easy prey for Blisters Schultz, had he not already started home.

Marius Tollman's money had shortened the odds on Amberezzio, but he was still returned at twelve to one. Marius Tollman wheezed and puffed from pay-out window to pay-out window, collecting his winnings bit by bit. He hadn't room for all the cash in the underarm pockets and finally stowed some casually in more accessible spots. Too bad about Blisters Schultz.

Fred Collyer collected a fistful of winnings and repaid the twenty to Clay Petrovitch.

'If you had a hot tip, you might have passed it on,' grumbled Petrovitch, thinking of all the expenses old Fred would undoubtedly claim for his free rides to the racecourse.

'It wasn't a tip, just a hunch.' He couldn't tell Clay what the hunch was, as he wrote for a rival paper. 'I'll buy you a drink on the way home.'

'I should damn well think so.'

Fred Collyer immediately regretted his offer, which had been instinctive. He remembered that he had not intended to drink until after he had written. Still, perhaps one . . . And he did need a drink very badly. It seemed a century since his last, on Wednesday night.

They left together, walking out with the remains of the crowd. The racecourse looked battered and bedraggled at the end of the day: the scarlet petals of the tulips lay on the ground, leaving rows of naked pistils sticking forlornly up, and the bright rugs of grass were dusty grey and covered with litter. Fred Collyer thought only of the dough in his pocket and the story in his head, and both of them gave him a nice warm glow.

A drink to celebrate, he thought. Buy Clay a thank-you drink, and maybe perhaps just one more to celebrate. It wasn't often, after all, that things fell his way so miraculously.

They stopped for the drink. The first double swept through Fred Collyer's veins like fire through a parched forest. The second made him feel great.

'Time to go,' he said to Clay. 'I've got my piece to write.'

'Just one more,' Clay said. 'This one's on me.'

'Better not.' He felt virtuous.

'Oh, come on,' Clay said, and ordered. With the faintest of misgivings Fred Collyer sank his third: but couldn't he still outwrite every racing man in the business? Of course he could.

They left after the third. Fred Collyer bought a fifth of Bourbon for later, when he had finished his story. Back in his own room he took just the merest swig from it before he sat down to write.

The words wouldn't come. He screwed up six attempts and poured some Bourbon into a tooth glass.

Marius Tollman, Crinkle Cut, Piper Boles, Amberezzio . . . It wasn't all that simple.

He took a drink. He didn't seem to be able to help it.

The Sports Editor would give him a raise for a story like this, or at least there would be no more quibbling about expenses.

He took a drink.

Piper Boles had earned himself a thousand bucks for crashing into Salad Bowl. Now how the hell did you write that without being sued for libel?

He took a drink.

The jockeys in the tenth race had conspired together to let the only straight one among them win. How in hell could you say that?

He took a drink.

The stewards and the press had had all their attention channelled towards the crash in the Derby and had virtually ignored the tenth race. The stewards wouldn't thank him for pointing it out.

He took another drink. And another. And more.

His deadline for telephoning his story to the office was ten o'clock the following morning. When that hour struck he was asleep and snoring, fully dressed, on his bed. The empty Bourbon bottle lay on the floor beside him, and his winnings, which he had tried to count, lay scattered over his chest.

READ MORE IN PENGUIN

For complete information about books available from Penguin and how to order them, please write to us at the appropriate address below. Please note that for copyright reasons the selection of books varies from country to country.

IN THE UNITED KINGDOM: Please write to *Dept. JC, Penguin Books Ltd, FREEPOST, West Drayton, Middlesex UB7 OBR.*
If you have any difficulty in obtaining a title, please send your order with the correct money, plus ten per cent for postage and packaging, to *PO Box No. 11, West Drayton, Middlesex UB7 OBR.*

IN THE UNITED STATES: Please write to *Consumer Sales, Penguin USA, P.O. Box 999, Dept. 17109, Bergenfield, New Jersey 07621-0120.* VISA and MasterCard holders call 1-800-253-6476 to order all Penguin titles.

IN CANADA: Please write to *Penguin Books Canada Ltd, 10 Alcorn Avenue, Suite 300, Toronto, Ontario M4V 3B2.*

IN AUSTRALIA: Please write to *Penguin Books Australia Ltd, P.O. Box 257, Ringwood, Victoria 3134.*

IN NEW ZEALAND: Please write to *Penguin Books (NZ) Ltd, Private Bag 102902, North Shore Mail Centre, Auckland 10.*

IN INDIA: Please write to *Penguin Books India Pvt Ltd, 706 Eros Apartments, 56 Nehru Place, New Delhi 110 019.*

IN THE NETHERLANDS: Please write to *Penguin Books Netherlands bv, Postbus 3507, NL-1001 AH Amsterdam.*

IN GERMANY: Please write to *Penguin Books Deutschland GmbH, Metzlerstrasse 26, 60594 Frankfurt am Main.*

IN SPAIN: Please write to *Penguin Books S. A., Bravo Murillo 19, 1o B, 28015 Madrid.*

IN ITALY: Please write to *Penguin Italia s.r.l., Via Felice Casati 20, I-20124 Milano.*

IN FRANCE: Please write to *Penguin France S. A., 17 rue Lejeune, F-31000 Toulouse.*

IN JAPAN: Please write to *Penguin Books Japan, Ishikiribashi Building, 2-5-4, Suido, Bunkyo-ku, Tokyo 112.*

IN GREECE: Please write to *Penguin Hellas Ltd, Dimocritou 3, GR-106 71 Athens.*

IN SOUTH AFRICA: Please write to *Longman Penguin Southern Africa (Pty) Ltd, Private Bag X08, Bertsham 2013.*